Richard Morgan

Well Done!

W9-APR-998

BARRON'S

I can dress
to play
outside...

...all by myself.

I can ride
my bike
to go
and hide...

...all by myself.

Well done!

I can wash my hands
in time for lunch...

I can
scoop up peas
and drink
my punch...

...all by
   myself.

Well done!

I can hold it,

so I don't miss...

...all by
myself.

Well done!

I can *hug* and
I can *kiss*,
but I need
YOU
to do this!

I like to try to do things
all by myself. Sometimes, though,
I do things a little wrong.
Now and then, I do things a lot
wrong.... But by trying, I grow
a lot and this makes my mommy
and daddy very happy.
And then I can do
even more things
ALL BY MYSELF!

Charlie
x

For Isobel,
the non-stop chatterbox.